This book should be returned to any branch of the
Lancashire County Library on or before the date shown

1 8 AUG 2016

Lancashire
County
Council

LL1(A)

ReadZone Books Limited

First published in this edition 2015

© in this edition ReadZone Books Limited 2015
© in text Paul Harrison 2005
© in illustrations Ruth Rivers 2005

British Library Cataloguing in Publication Data (CIP) is available
for this title.

Printed in Malta by Melita Press.

ISBN 978 1 78322 470 8

Visit our website: www.readzonebooks.com

The Disappearing Cheese

by Paul Harrison

illustrated by Ruth Rivers

READZONE

One night a foolish man was
walking past the sea.
His tummy was as empty
as his head.

So when he looked out to sea, he thought, "My, look at that cheese under the water.
I'll have that!"

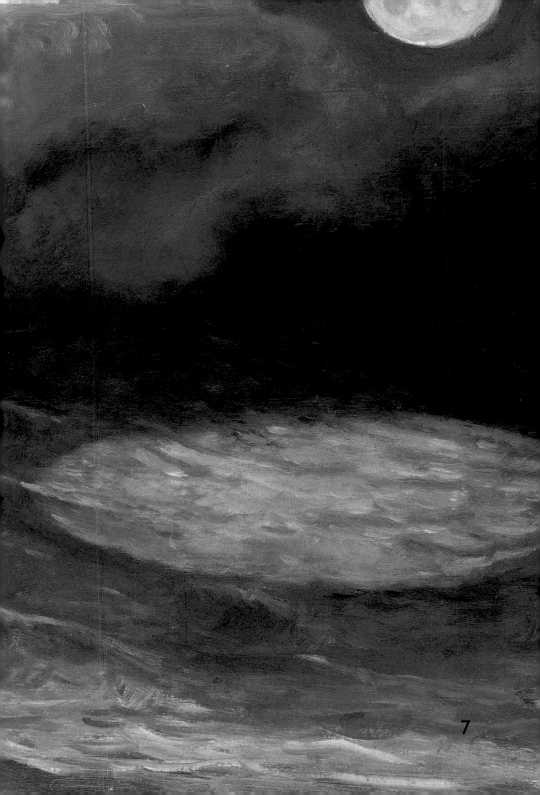

He reached out,
but the cheese moved.

He waded into the water,
but the cheese
moved again.

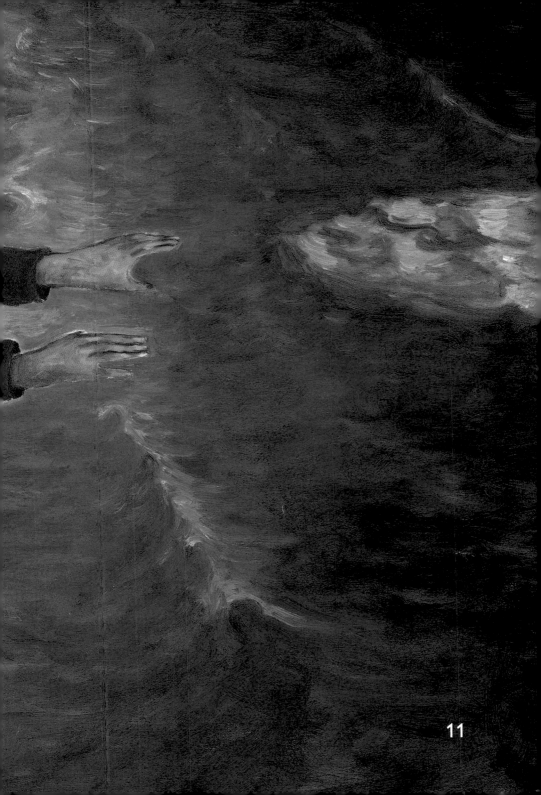

So home he went.

"Wife, come and help me catch a cheese."

But they couldn't catch it.

So home they went.

"Daughter, come and help us catch a cheese."

But still they couldn't catch it.

So home they went.

"Dog, come and help us catch a cheese."

But still they couldn't catch it.

"We need a boat," said the
man.

So off they went to
fetch a boat.

And they chased the cheese all over the sea...

...until a big cloud made
the cheese disappear.

"Ah well," said the man,
"I don't like cheese anyway."

Did you enjoy this book?

Look out for more *Magpies* titles –
fun stories in 150 words

The Clumsy Cow by Julia Moffat and Lisa Williams
ISBN 978 1 78322 157 8

The Disappearing Cheese by Paul Harrison and Ruth Rivers
ISBN 978 1 78322 470 8

Flying South by Alan Durant and Kath Lucas
ISBN 978 1 78322 410 4

Fred and Finn by Madeline Goodey and Mike Gordon
ISBN 978 1 78322 411 1

Growl! by Vivian French and Tim Archbold
ISBN 978 1 78322 412 8

I Wish I Was an Alien by Vivian French and Lisa Williams
ISBN 978 1 78322 413 5

Lovely, Lovely Pirate Gold by Scoular Anderson
ISBN 978 1 78322 206 3

Pet to School Day by Hilary Robinson and Tim Archbold
ISBN 978 1 78322 471 5

Tall Tilly by Jillian Powell and Tim Archbold
ISBN 978 1 78322 414 2

Terry the Flying Turtle by Anna Wilson and Mike Gordon
ISBN 978 1 78322 415 9

Too Small by Kay Woodward and Deborah van de Leijgraaf
ISBN 978 1 78322 156 1

Turn Off the Telly by Charlie Gardner and Barbara Nascimbeni
ISBN 978 1 78322 158 5